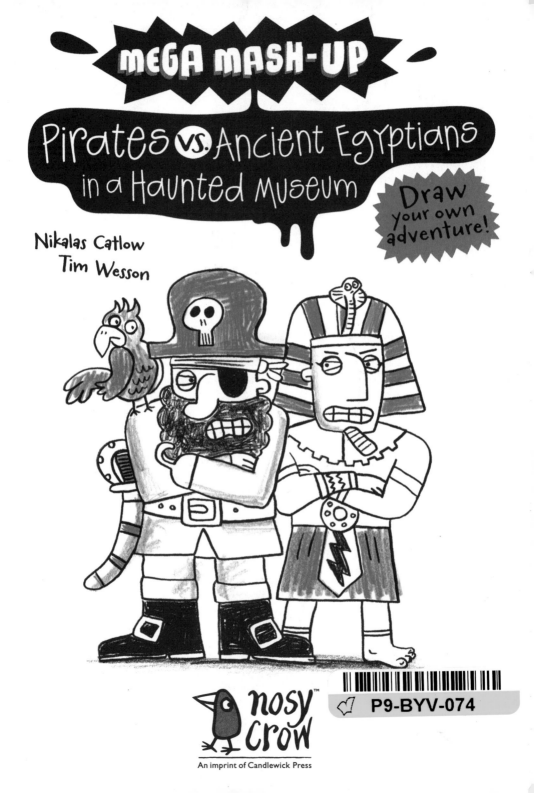

MEGA MASH-UP

Pirates vs. Ancient Egyptians in a Haunted Museum

Draw your own adventure!

Nikalas Catlow
Tim Wesson

nosy crow
An imprint of Candlewick Press

An imprint of Candlewick Press

First U.S. edition 2012

Library of Congress Cataloging-in-Publication Data is available.

Library of Congress Catalog Card Number pending

ISBN 978-0-7636-5901-1

12 13 14 15 16 17 BVG 10 9 8 7 6 5 4 3 2 1

Printed in Berryville, VA, U.S.A.

This book was typeset in Agenda.
The illustrations were created digitally.

Nosy Crow
an imprint of
Candlewick Press
99 Dover Street
Somerville, Massachusetts 02144

www.nosycrow.com
www.candlewick.com

Your hand

This book needs

YOU!

What if some bloodthirsty **Pirates** and crazy **Ancient Egyptians** broke into a HAUNTED MUSEUM?

Would one of them STEAL the PRICELESS GOLDEN HOWLER MONKEY?

Or would the museum's SPOOKY **GHOSTS** turn against them first?

You'll have to finish the illustrations and find out. . . .

Prepare to **LAUGH** while you doodle and SNICKER while you read.

Visit our awesome website and get involved!

www.megamash-up.com

Upload artwork and get the latest news.

Introducing the Pirates!

★ Bloodythirsty Jack ★

★ Scurvy Sid ★

★ Captain Curse ★

★ Beardy Belinda ★

★ Pete the Plank ★

Introducing the Ancient Egyptians!

★ Niles ★

★ Pharo-Nuff ★

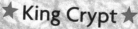
★ King Crypt ★

★ Marvin the Mummy ★

★ Bird-Head Horace ★

You'll need these . . .

DRAWING tools

These are the **3** tools
that Nikalas and Tim used
to create the artwork in
this book.

felt-tip pen or marker

pencil

crayon

Using different
tools helps create
great drawings.

texture page

pen zigzags

crayon rubbing from linoleum floor

pencil cross-hatching

crayon rubbing from wood floor

pencil rubbing from wooden door

scribbly pencil

There are lots of ways you can add texture to your artwork. Here are a few examples.

crayon rubbing from wall

pencil dashes

DRAWING TIP! Turn to the back of the book for ideas on stuff you might want to draw in this adventure.

pen circles

Chapter 1

Monkey Business!

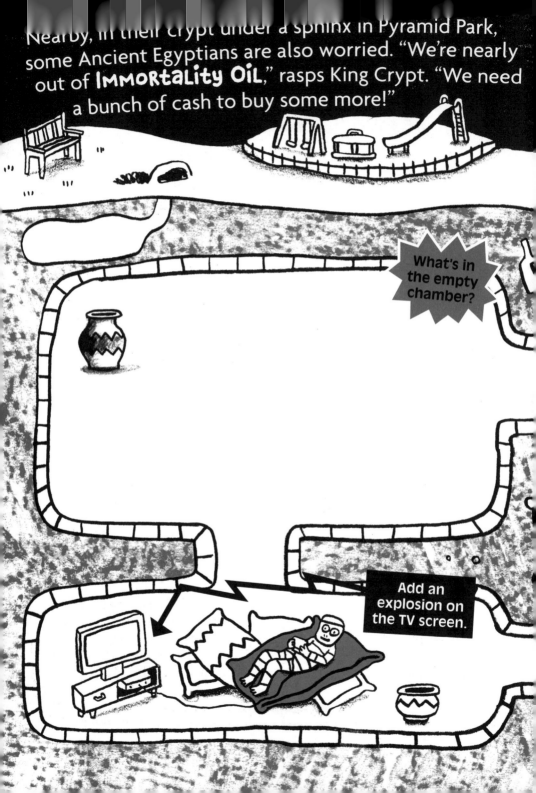

Design a throne fit for a king.

Yuck! Marvin the Mummy keeps his brain in a jar by the bed.

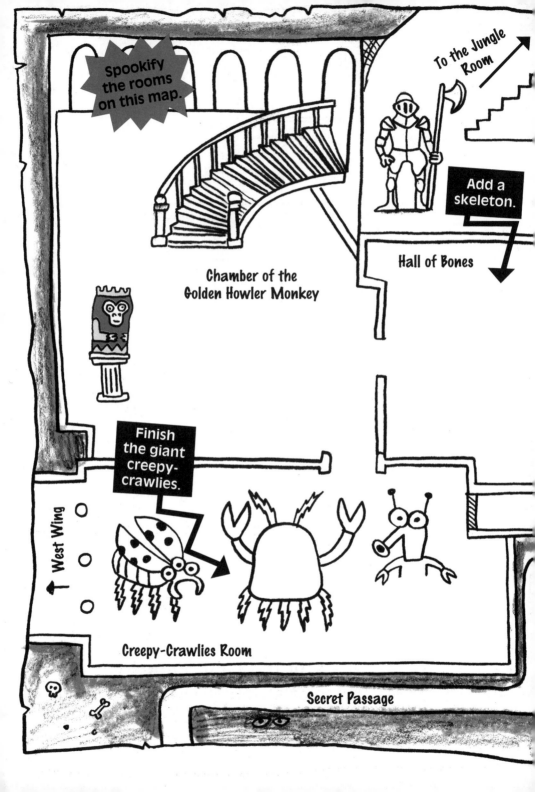

The Pirates and the Ancient Egyptians both have maps of the town's **abandoned** museum. Somewhere inside lies a priceless statue of a Golden Howler Monkey. Whoever steals it will be **MEGA-RICH**! But they must be quick — the museum is due to be demolished today!

East Wing

Chamber of Horrors

Spooky Cellar

The Ancient Egyptians are getting ready to rob the museum, too. "Anyone **NEED THE BATHROOM** before we go?" asks King Crypt.

The Pirates pile onto the Number 42 bus.
"Take us to the museum as fast as ye can, driver," growls Captain Curse. "Or we'll scuttle this bus!"
"That'll be $2.80," replies the driver, **COOL AS CUSTARD**.

Who will get into the museum first?
Who will find the priceless
Golden Howler Monkey? And who
will be scared witless by the
museum's **SPOOKY** residents?

Add more bats to spooky up the sky!

That doesn't sound very friendly!

Chapter 2
Night at the Museum

The Pirates decide to break into the museum through the sewers. "Arrr! This place be **STINKIER** than Scurvy Sid's socks!" cries Pete the Plank.

The Ancient Egyptians arrive at the museum, too. “We’ll SNEAK in through the basement,” whispers King Crypt. “Ignore those signs — no one’s going to knock down the museum today!”
What do these signs say?
DUE FOR DEMOLITION TODAY

The Pirates pop up through the museum's toilets.
"We made it, **mateys!**" splutters Captain Curse,
waving a toilet-paper roll around victoriously.

"Now, let's go find us a Golden Howler Monkey!"

"Yikes!" shrieks Marvin the Mummy.
"**SLUDGE MONSTERS!**"

What's lurking in the stinky basement?

BASEMENT

Woooo! Add a spooky trapdoor.

"Yikes!" shrieks Scurvy Sid. "**A moldy old Mummy!**"
"We're black-hearted Pirates, 'ere to grab us the
Golden Howler Monkey!" announces Captain Curse.
"We're noble Ancient Egyptians," says King Crypt
snootily. "And the monkey will be yours over my
   embalmed body!"

After **fighting** for five minutes, they make a pact. "Right, ye poxy old landlubbers," says Captain Curse. "You take that door, and we'll take this 'un. Whosoever finds the Golden Howler Monkey first keeps it."

Add an Oof! sound effect.

Chapter 3

Exhibit A-aaagghh!

The Pirates consult their map. "Oh, no! We gotta go through the **CREEPY-CRAWLIES** room," exclaims Beardy Belinda. "And look — they're wriggling through the door!"

Make this door even more CREEPY!

Nervously, the Pirates go inside.
BUZZ! SWISH! SWOOOSH!
The creepy-crawlies are **attacking**!

Meanwhile, the Ancient Egyptians have reached the Jungle Room. "What weird plants!" says Pharo-Nuff. "I must go closer . . . **AAAAGGGHHHH**!" Something has grabbed his ancient ankle. It's a monster vine!

What else is in the Jungle Room?

BASH

Add more texture to the monster vine.

Strange Sounds, suspiciously like singing, can be heard from below: "ALL RIGHT! EVERYBODY IN THE HOUSE SAY 'YEAH'!"

What sounds is the Golden Howler Monkey making?

CREAK, CRACK, CRASH! Pharo-Nuff has
CRASHED through a hole in the floor.
"I can see the **GOLDEN HOWLER MONKEY**!"
he yells. "And I can almost reach it!"

But the Pirates have reached the Chamber of the Golden Howler Monkey, too. "I can hear singing behind that door!" cries Beardy Belinda, tapping her **HAiRY toe**.

"**FOLLOW THAT TUNE!**" orders Captain Curse.
    "The Golden Howler Monkey is nigh!"

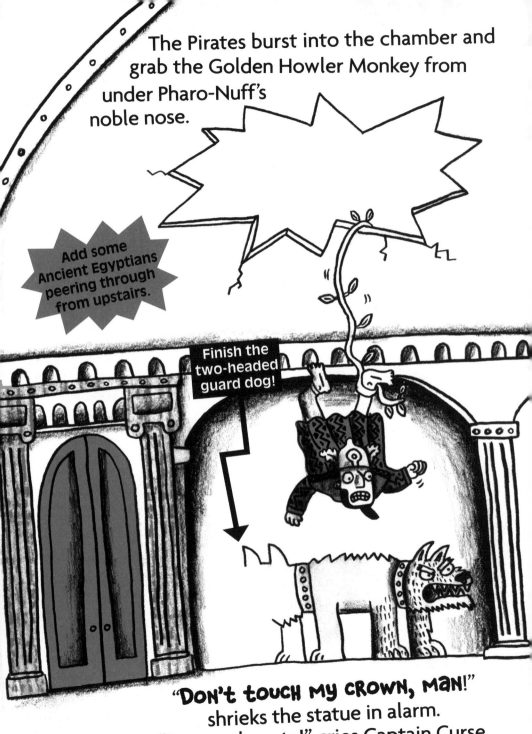

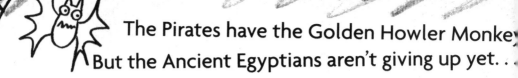

The Pirates have the Golden Howler Monkey.
But the Ancient Egyptians aren't giving up yet. . .

Chapter 4

Name That Tune!

The stairs dump the Pirates back into the Chamber of the Golden Howler Monkey. "Serves you **scallywags** right," the Ancient Egyptians cry, snatching the priceless statue. "We're rich! RICH!"

The Ancient Egyptians run into the next room with the Golden Howler Monkey. "Holy camel, it's **C-C-COLD** in here," complains Bird-Head Horace. "Must be the **Ice Age**!"

Draw a mammoth on the rampage.

Exhausted and dizzy, the Pirates rush out of the tunnel into a room full of shrunken heads. " 'Ave you seen any thievin' **OLD geezeRS** wiv a Golden Howler Monkey?" Beardy Belinda asks one of them.

Add more heads on the plinths.

He's a real nobody. Tee-hee!

"Over there," it groans in reply. "Past the stuffed BEAR with one arm." In all the excitement, no one hears a **bulldozer** starting its engine. . . .

Scribble-texture the bear.

Who's grinning in the mirror?

"There's one of them!" gurgles Scurvy Sid, pointing at a disappearing Ancient Egyptian. "Aaargh! Look at that ARMCHAIR! It's got eyes and teeth. Grab an ax — we'll 'ave to hack our way through!"

"**My bandages**!" he shrieks. "I'm unraveling!"
"Hang in there, Marvin," shouts Bird-Head Horace.
"I'll pry his **bony fingers** off with my crook."

But what's this?
SMASH! The bulldozers have started to demolish the museum. **CRASH!** Down comes a huge dinosaur's **Rib cage** and traps the Ancient Egyptians.

Add a prehistoric rib cage crashing down on the Ancient Egyptians.

Wow! The shattered skull of a T. rex!

"What a bunch of BONEHEADS!" scoffs Captain Curse. "Now, we'll be 'avin' that Golden Howler Monkey, thankin' you kindly!"

The museum is being smashed to its foundations!
The dinosaur's rib cage splits apart.
The walls are crumbling, and plaster
is **falling** from the ceilings.

Finish the scene of ultimate destruction.

Add a big bulldozer.

CHapter 5
Stars in Their Eyes

Amazingly, everyone survives the demolition in one piece! Once the dust has settled, a tug-of-war begins.

"The monkey is mine!" shouts Captain Curse.
"No, it's mine! Mine! Mine!" hollers King Crypt.
But the Golden Howler Monkey has **HaD eNOuGH**. . . .

What lies buried beneath their feet?

A suit of armor

The museum safe

"Stop it, all of you!" it yells. "There's something you need to know."

An old motorbike

"I'm only made of **FAKE** gold, so stealing me won't make you rich," explains the Golden Howler Monkey. "But my singing is priceless! Let's start a band and become rich and famous rock stars!"

The Golden Howler Monkey is picturing his name in showbiz lights.

They are imagining what it would be like to be famous.

"There's lots of stuff in the rubble we can use as instruments," says Pharo-Nuff. "Let's get digging! We'll call ourselves **THE SPOOKY CREW**!"

What has Pharo-Nuff found to use as an instrument?

What has King Crypt pulled out of that hole?

Finish the chiming heads.

Decorate the wall with pictures of pop stars.

Soon, they have a record deal. And a manager.
"Hey, guys," says Simon Towel. "I love your act.
I'm gonna make you **SUPERSTARS!**"

Chapter 6
That's Showbiz!

The band is ready to go on tour! All aboard the **SPOOKY CREW** mean machine!

Make the tour bus super cool.

"Everyone on the bus go 'AHHHHHH'!" yells the Golden Howler Monkey. "Put the pedal to the metal!" And they're off!

When the Spooky Crew arrives, some fans spot them. "Awesome!" the fans **SCREAM**, chasing the band down the street.

This fan has a crazed look in her eye.

This fan is dressed like Marv.

Draw an ad for something REALLY COOL here!

The Spooky Crew is a massive hit.
It's show time! The **fans** go wild!

Add more
Spooky Crew
fans.

"And our treasure chests be overflowin' with **Pieces of eight!**" cries Captain Curse, his new gold teeth flashing in the sun.

Design a Pirate dollar bill.

What a **SPECTACULARLY** spooky time they all had at the Haunted Museum! "We found the Golden Howler Monkey!" says Captain Curse.
"We met a saber-toothed tiger," King Crypt chimes in.

"Then the museum fell on our heads!" adds Pharo-Nuff. "But best of all," concludes the Golden Howler Monkey, "we became mega-superstars!"

Picture Glossary

If you get stuck or need ideas,
then use these pages for reference.

SKATEBOARDS

BOTTOM VIEW

TOP VIEW

SEWER MONSTER

If you like, you can copy the pictures. OR you can draw your own versions.

SHOWING OFF

THE MUSEUM'S GUIDE

ANGRY

HI THERE!

SHOCKED

More Picture Glossary

SAFE

A SKULL AFTER AN ARGUMENT WITH A PIRATE

MAMMOTHS

WITH VICTIM

Nikalas's MAMMOTH

MAD

WITHOUT VICTIM

Tim's MAMMOTH

HOPPING MAD

Visit our **awesome** website and get involved!

Website

MEGA MASH-UP

My Mash-up | Mega Draw | The Books | Ask Us | What's Next?

OUT NOW!

The first two books in the series

Click here to audition a character for our next book!

Click here to see our Mega Picture Glossary!

Breaking News!
This just in - a Haunted Museum is to be the scene of the next Mega Mash-Up! It's thought that some Pirates and some Ancient Egyptians will have a bit of a barney and CHAOS and MAYHEM will ensue! There'll be mummies

www.megamash-up.com
Upload artwork and get the latest news.